A Lost Lana

By Mimi Mae

Chapter 1

It was just another day in the life of an average family. Olivia was just a normal 11-year-old girl, her 9-year-old brother Jack, was the typical annoying younger brother.
They lived in a cottage by the sea with their mother, Emma.

Olivia and Jack were always fighting about something, anything, everything!
On this occasion it was

who was going to answer the door to a strange knock.

"I'll get it" Said Olivia,

"NO!! I want to" shouted Jack.

"You always do it" argued Olivia.

"No, you did it last time" Jack stated.

While they were having their usual shouting match over who was going to answer the door, their mother sighed "Those kids drive me mad, will they ever agree about anything", and with that she went to see who was at the door.

BANG!!!!!

Olivia and Jack stopped arguing and stared at each other in silence for a second… "what was that?" said Jack worriedly.

"I don't know," exclaimed Olivia, "Let's go and find out!" They both ran to the front door only to find there was no one there….

Chapter 2

"Where did mum go?" shouted Jack nervously, "Mum!! Mum!!! He yelled, hoping for some sort of reply.
"This is really weird" said Olivia, "she was here a second ago, and now she's gone". "If we are going to find mum, we need to work together for once and not argue about everything" Olivia explained to Jack. "Can you do that?" she asked.

"Yes!" Jack said with tears welling up in his eyes, "We just need to find mum". "So where do we start?" questioned Jack.

"Well, mum answered the door and now she has disappeared." Olivia replied, pausing to think "So maybe if we opened the door too, we would end up in the same place as mum!".

They both agreed and looked over at the front door. "here goes nothing" said Olivia nervously while slowly turning the door handle.

Chapter 3

Olivia slowly opened her eyes. "What happened, where am I" she thought to herself. As her eyes opened fully she saw Jack laying next to her. "Jack, Jack wake up!" she shouted as she shook him gently. After a few gentle shakes, Jacks eyes opened, and he slowly woke up.

"what happened, where are we" he asked Olivia.

"That's what I was thinking" she said. "Did it

work? Have we found mum? Jack said excitedly.

"I don't think so" Olivia said, her voice gently shaking with nerves "we have a long way to go yet".
They both looked around. They were standing in a strange room with gold, diamonds, and all sorts of other jewels frozen solid in walls and a ceiling of clear ice. From the Ceiling hung beautiful crystal chandeliers.

"Wow!" Olivia shouted, "this is beautiful!".

"Yes, but where is mum?" asked Jack unimpressed by the beautiful room around him.

"you're right" said Olivia, "we need to focus."

They looked around the room, "is there a way out?" said Jack, "I don't see a door."

"well mum's not here, so she must have got out somehow" Olivia said rather cleverly.

"look! Over there…in the corner" shouted Jack happily, "I see a light!" He started to run towards it

“I’m going to get there first!”

“Jack!!” Olivia shouted after him “wait for me, we are supposed to be working together remember!!” Remembering his earlier agreement, he slowed to let Olivia catch up

“yeah ok, sorry” he moaned.

The light was coming from what looked like a hole in the wall.

As they both got closer to the hole, they noticed the room getter bigger and bigger. As they passed through the hole in the wall, the light disappeared.

Chapter 4

Once the bright light had dulled, and their eyes had a chance to focus, they looked around them and saw that they were in another room.
" Are we in another house?" Jack asked, confused.

"I….I think so" said Olivia, still trying to work it out. "It looks like a dolls house….hang on…this looks like MY DOLLS HOUSE!!" She shouted, suddenly realising what had happened. "Jack, remember when we were in that last room and we thought it was getting bigger? Well I think it was actually us getting smaller and we have been shrunk down so small that we are now in my dolls house!"

Jack looked around and saw things he recognised from Olivia's room

"How did this happen?" he said, "and more importantly…how do we fix it!" "I don't know" said Olivia, still trying to understand it all. "let's just focus on finding mum, and then we can sort this out". As they walked around the doll's house it became clear what had happened. It was Olivia's dolls house, they were in her room and they had shrunk to a tiny size.

Chapter 5

As they walked through the doll's house together, they held each other close. All the dolls had changed, they were not only bigger than the pair of them, they were now spooky looking too.

They had red bloodshot eyes, pale faces, and messy hair. Some had what look like blood running down them and stains on their now torn clothes.

"This is terrifying!" cried Jack

"I know," replied Olivia "my poor dolls, what's happened to them?"

They continued on through the different rooms until they reached the edge of the doll's house. They stopped and stared out across Olivia's bedroom. It looked huge, the drop to the floor alone was like looking into the Grand Canyon!

"what the hell are we meant to do now?" asked Jack with a hopeless tone to his voice "how do we get out when we can't even get down to the floor?"

"Calm down!" shouted Olivia "we just need to take a deep breath and think about it. Something will come to us!"

Chapter 6

They stood at the edge of the doll's house, perched close to the edge of the unit the doll's house sat on. Both were searching the room for ideas on how to get down.

"Got it!" Jack suddenly shouted "we can use your yo-yo! We can put one end in the doll's house and then slide down the string! It's perfect!" he yelled triumphantly.

"hmmm great idea, but with one tiny problem"

replied Olivia "what's that over there on the middle shelf?" she asked Jack.

"It's your yo-yo" answered Jack, suddenly realising that actually getting to the yo-yo was impossible, let alone using it.

"Wait!" said Olivia as she run over to the side of the unit and looked down "YES!" she screamed with excitement "Jack I've got it, come here quick" she continued "mum disappeared before doing the laundry, which means my pile of clothes is still there! We can use it as a soft landing and jump down," she explained to Jack who was looking very scared about the whole thing and not at all excited about the huge jump

"No way am I jumping all that way to land in your smelly clothes!" he said, "There might be smelly old socks in there!"

"Oh don't be silly," Olivia replied getting ready to jump "well I'm doing it and unless you have any better ideas it's our only option."

Realising she was right, Jack came round to the idea and asked Olivia rather embarrassed

"will you hold my hand?"

"Of course I will! We are a team remember?" Olivia replied doing her best to comfort Jack who was clearly terrified.

"Ok, Ready? On three" suggested Olivia, they both looked at each other and nodded.
"....One.....Two...Three!!"

As Olivia shouted "Three" they both leaped into the pile of clothes.

Chapter 7

Olivia and Jack both lay in one of Olivia's smelly socks.

"urgh, that stinks" complained Jack "I knew we would land in your smelly socks" Jack moaned holding his nose.

"Well it's a pile of laundry" replied Olivia "of course it's going to have smelly socks in it, yours does too!"

They both look at each other and burst into a fit of

laughter, rolling around in the smelly socks which no longer seem to bother Jack.

"shhh," Olivia suddenly stops laughing and looks serious "what's that noise?"

"I hear it too" claims Jack

"HIDE! someone's coming" They both shout.

They hide behind the leg of the unit they just jumped off, and they carefully peer around it to try and see what's coming.

Olivia suddenly notices a small black nose poking through the door.

"COCO!" she screamed, "Jack it's Coco"

Coco was their puppy, a small, light caramel coloured dog, with fluffy fur.

Chapter 8

Olivia was happy but also a bit scared that Coco may not recognise them and see them as food.
"Stay here Jack, she might not recognise us being so small" said Olivia as she pushed Jack back behind the leg of the unit they were hiding behind.

"Of course she will! COCO! COCO! Jack shouted as loud as he could.

Coco looked over toward them and started to trot

over. As she arrived, she seemingly recognised them straight away and started to sniff and lick them. As lovely as this was, it was also quite scary as her tongue was now much larger than both Olivia and Jack together.

"She must recognise our smell" claimed Olivia.

"Yeah, the smell of your socks!" laughed Jack, this made them both laugh again.

Now they knew Coco recognised them, and

hadn't changed like the dolls had done, they were much more relaxed.

"Hey," Olivia suddenly says, "maybe Coco can sniff out mum?"

"Great Idea!" Jack said, "but we won't be able to keep up with her if she runs off looking for her" Jack says realising how small they are compared to the dog.

"We'll have to ride on her" Olivia said, already hatching a plan "Coco sit!!" she shouts as loud as she can so Coco can hear her.

The fluffy dog sits down and places her head into the carpet.

"Quickly," shouts Olivia "climb up her tail and onto her back."

The pair climb aboard Coco and Olivia shouts in her ear

"Coco, go find mum!"

Chapter 9

Coco starts to run towards the door of Olivia's bedroom.

"Woah," said Olivia, "this is not easy, hold on tight Jack!" she shouted as Coco picked up speed.

"I'm trying!" Jack shouted back, "but it's not easy!"

As Coco started to jump down each step, Olivia and Jack struggled to hold on. Each step was like trying to hang on to a raging bull during an earthquake.

"Help!!!" came the shout all of a sudden from behind Olivia. She turned around to see Jack hanging on to Coco's fur on the side of her. He had fallen off but managed to grab her fur at the last minute.

"hang on Jack!" Screamed Olivia, desperately trying to hold on herself.

Olivia started to move slowly down to where Jack was and shouted to him to take her hand.

"I....I can't!" shouted Jack while gripping as tight as he could to Coco.

Olivia slid down a bit more,

"How about now?" she shouted.
Jack looked up at her, Olivia could see how frightened he was.

"You have to trust me Jack, you can do this" she yelled in the most supportive way she could.

Jack took a deep breath, and with every effort he could, he reached for Olivia's hand. Olivia grabbed him and with all the strength she had she pulled him back up.

Just as they got back up on to Coco's back, they reached the bottom of the stairs and all became a lot calmer.

Once at the bottom of the stairs, Coco heads towards the living room but suddenly stops by the 'mouse hole' in the entrance hall.

"What is it girl" asks Olivia "What can you smell? Is it mum?" Coco ruffs a little bark and lays down in front of hole.

"I think we should investigate" says Jack, "what do you think partner?"

Olivia looks at Jack in amazement, maybe this whole thing was bringing them closer together.

"I think you're right" she replies, "it looks like Coco can smell something!" They both lower themselves off Coco's back and walk slowly towards the mouse hole.

Chapter 10

Olivia and Jack approach the hole with caution. As they get closer, they can hear voices, but they don't sound human. They are deep and gravely sounding.

They peer through the hole and can see a dark room. It was difficult to see much as it was all black apart from a few candles.
The candles lit up a circle of what were troll like creatures. They were

stood in a large circle surrounding a person tied up in the middle, the person looked liked....

"MUM!!" said Jack rather too loudly.

"what was that?" said one of the trolls, "It came from over there" he pointed to where Jack and Olivia were standing.
"shhhhhh!! Be quiet" whispered Olivia pushing her finger to Jacks lips.

"quick, we need to hide" Olivia says jumping back on to Coco. Jack joins her and they shout to Coco to run to the cupboard under the stairs.

Coco squeezes through the door of the cupboard and lays down. Olivia and Jack peer through the door to see if they were followed.

Meanwhile, the trolls had come to the edge of the mouse hole to see who had made the noise. They were all holding large sticks, with tops that glowed an orangey red looking colour.

"There's no one out here, you must have been

hearing things" said one of the trolls, "come on, let's go" said another as they disappeared back into the hole.

Olivia turned to Jack and said, "we've found her! but how do we save her?"

Jack had a blank expression on his face.

"hmmm" he said, "I have an idea".

Chapter 11

Jack begins to tell Olivia about his plan.
"remember when we were scared of Coco because she was so big compared to us? Well, she's huge to the trolls as well! If we could get the trolls to come out of the hole, we can scare them with Coco! Then while they are being scared, we can run in and get mum!"

"That's a fantastic idea" Olivia said excitedly,

"how on earth did you think of that?"

"what can I say" he said with a big grin on his face "sometimes I'm brilliant!" they both giggled.

After sorting out a few last details of their plan, Jack and Olivia walked over to the hole.

They stood right outside it and started talking loudly so the trolls would hear them.

"Hello in there!" they both shouted

"we are coming to save our mum and there's

nothing you can do to stop us!" Olivia shouted

"Yeah, we are stronger and smarter than you!" added Jack.

The trolls inside all looked at each other puzzled.

"stronger than us?" said one of them, "we'll see about that! Trolls, all of you attack!" he called.

All the trolls came out of the hole ready to attack. However, when they saw Olivia and Jack standing there they stopped, looked at each other and back to Olivia and Jack.

“where are they?” shouted one of the trolls to Olivia and Jack. “the people that are stronger and smarter than us?”

“That’s us,” said Olivia calmly.

The trolls began to grin an evil grin and started to walk toward Olivia and Jack.

“we will see about that” said the troll

“Yes, we will” smirked Olivia “Coco now!!” she shouted.

Coco came running out of the cupboard under the

stairs and stood in front of Olivia and Jack, growling and showing her huge teeth to the trolls.

"Run away!!" shouted the trolls and they all run in different directions.

In the confusion Olivia and Jack run into the hole and untie their mum.

"I'm so glad to see you both" she said as they all embrace in a big cuddle.

"Quick, lets get out of here" mum said suddenly realising they were still in danger. They all nod and run out of the hole.

Chapter 12

Once out of the hole, they call to Coco.

"Coco, here girl!" shouts Olivia.

Coco comes over and lays in front of them and they all climb up her tail and aboard her back.

"to my room Coco" said Olivia.

Coco runs back up to Olivia's room with the family holding on tightly to avoid falling again.

Once back in Olivia's room Coco walks over to the dolls house and the family all walk off.

"good girl!" Olivia says to Coco "such a good girl".

"right, now what!" said Jack "we are still tiny and it's getting late, we can't spend the rest of our lives in a dolls house. I've got school tomorrow!" his eyes were beginning to tear as he suddenly realised he didn't know what to do now.

"well," said mum calmly, "I find that when I don't

know what to do next, I go back to the beginning and start again."

Both Olivia and Jack stared at their mum with open mouths.

"we are not going through that again!" Olivia said with Jack nodding in agreement.

"No," mum laughed "I meant retrace your steps, work in reverse" the kids still looked at her puzzled.

"eh?" Jack sighed "I think the trolls banged her on the head" he said scratching his head.

“oh just follow me!” said mum thinking the best way was to show them what she meant rather than explain.

“when I opened the front door this morning I ended up in the dolls house” she said as she led Olivia and Jack through the doll’s house.

“yes, so did we” Olivia replied in agreement.

“Where did you go to in the doll’s house?” asked mum.

“erm,” Olivia started to think back to the morning

and remembered waking up next to Jack "it was in the bedroom on the left at the top of the house"

"me too" said mum, "maybe that means something.

As they all walked into the bedroom, they could see a wardrobe in the corner of the room with a glow around the doors.

"There!" Jack shouted "there's something in that wardrobe" he said excited but nervous at the same time.

“maybe it’s a way back?” Olivia said hopefully

“Only one way to find out” said mum positioning the children and herself in front of the wardrobe doors.

She opened the doors, and everything turned very bright white, so much so that they all had to close their eyes.

When they opened their eyes they were in the hall staring at the front door….back to normal size again!
“It worked!” screamed

Olivia and Jack together.
They all hugged tightly.

Chapter 13

The family all stood in the hallway hugging each other tightly, Coco was now joining in by running around their legs.

"Wait!" Olivia shouted suddenly, she ran up the stairs and came back down a few seconds later holding the small wardrobe they had gone through when they were tiny.

"I think we should destroy this so it can't happen again" she explained.

"I agree!" said Jack nodding.

They placed it on the floor and Jack stamped on it and broke it into lots of pieces.

"there, that's that done. Just one more thing to do" he said walking off towards the kitchen"

Olivia and mum looked at each other puzzled.

Jack returned a minute later with a small piece of wood, a hammer, and some nails.

“we need to block up that mouse hole!” he says, handing the stuff to mum.

Mum laughs and gets down on the floor, places the small piece of wood over the mouse hole and hammers the nails in place.

“there you go, all done” she says with a smile.

It had been a long day for the family, and after a quick bite to eat they all sat in the living talking about what they had done.

“you know, I’m so proud of you both” she said

pulling them both into a hug.

“you worked as a team today, you made finding me more important than arguing. I hope this means you are not going to argue anymore and be nicer to each other.

Olivia and Jack look at each other and smile.

“I’ll try to be nice” said Olivia

“and I’ll try to be less annoying” said Jack

“Jack!!” Olivia and mum shouted together.

They all laughed loudly as they continued talking about their day for a while longer before mum said

"time for bed, I'm sure you'll sleep well after such a busy day"
Jack and Olivia got ready for bed and before disappearing into their own rooms they looked at each other and smiled.

"Goodnight sis" said Jack

"Goodnight little brother" replied Olivia.

The End.

Printed in Great Britain
by Amazon

45562156R00038